This book belongs to ....

Sortland

Stokmarknes

Trollfjorden

Stamsund

Svolvær

Tromsø

Risøyhamn

Finnsnes

Harstad

Narvik

Hello! I am Little Sister, Julie. I come
from Tromsø, in the north of Norway. We have the
midnight sun. I am on my way to Svolvær on board
the Hurtigruten with my family. Lyra is always with
me. The two of us have looked forward to this trip.

Do you feel happy and excited whenever you're going on a trip?

Welcome aboard!

Here you can see Dad, Big Brother, Mum and Big Sister. They are always busy.
But now we are finally going to enjoy ourselves together on the Hurtigruten!

Hurry up inside and hop into bed – we have to get up early in the morning.

Ooh!
What a nice cabin

Good night!

Finnsnes 4.45am

Dad! Somebody has taken Lyra! Can you please help me?

Sorry, not just now. I've just started breakfast. Perhaps Mum can help you. She's always so helpful.

Hello darling! Sorry - not right now. I am busy training. You will have to ask your Big Sister for help.

Has this ever happened to you, that grown-ups are busy and that they don't have time for you?

Hello Little Sis! We are chatting with our friends on the Internet. Ask your brother.

Hey! Don't disturb me! I'm playing against the best football team in the world and I'm about to set a new record!

But Lyra is in danger!
You have to help me NOW!

Stop!
You can't go into the galley!
No, no, no!

Ok – let's grab some kitchen tools. The thief won't get away with this!

Oi! Look everyone!
A real troll holding Lyra in his arms.
What shall we do?

Can you find all of the soft toys hidden in the picture?

Help us to wake the troll. We will count to three
– then we have to shout as loud as we can! Ready? 1... 2... 3...

Sortland 1.00pm

Please, don't scare me! Why are you all so angry with me?

Because you stole our best friends!

I have lost my family that lives in Trollfjord.
So I took your soft toys just for some comfort and company.
I'm so sorry! Can you please forgive me?

Do you say "sorry" when you have done something naughty?
Do you forgive people that have been mean to you?

Now we understand everything! We are not angry with you anymore. Of course we forgive you. We will help you to find your family again. You can trust us!

Now, let's do something fun together! We can go to the gift shop and find you a soft toy of your own.

What's your name, by the way?
My name is Troll-Olav.

There you go, Troll-Olav!
Loffen is perfect for you.

He has a patch on his clothes too, just like you

Now, let's go and have some fun!

Come on, let's all go up on deck and jump in the jacuzzi!

Stokmarknes 3.15pm

This is so much fun!
Thank you for being
so kind to me!

Can you find Lyra and Loffen? Can you see the reindeer, dog, lamb, zebra, lynx, alpaca, and the panda?

Hurry up everybody!
We are sailing into Trollfjord.
Come, Troll-Olav, you will soon
meet your family again.

Look! Look!
Yahoo! - It's Troll-Olav!!!

Mr. Captain! You must stop the ship! I have to get off now.
I want to go home to my family. I live in Trollfjord, you see.

Svolvær 6.30pm

Well done, my friends! We have solved a big problem in a good way.

It feels nice making others happy.

Do you feel good when you make others happy?